Aditi
and the
One-Eyed Monkey

Suniti Namjoshi

art

Bindia Thapar

Tulika

1

The Ant and the Elephant

It was about ten in the morning in the middle of May. The one-eyed monkey had stopped leaping and loping and rambling through the countryside and had taken refuge in a shady neem tree. Everything was so hot and blazed so blindingly that the monkey fixed her gaze on the roots of the tree where a number of ants were busy working. 'O ants,' she said. 'Good Morning,' she shouted. 'Hot weather,' she yelled. But the ants didn't falter and not even one of them answered, 'Good Morning'.

The monkey felt irritated. She decided that she would somehow make them speak. She jumped off the tree and, having cleared a small space, she put a lump of sugar, which she happened to have, in the middle of it. An ant broke rank and was soon joined by nine other ants. As they were hoisting the lump on their shoulders, the monkey interrupted them.

'Just a minute. That lump of sugar belongs to me.'

'Oh no,' replied the ants, 'lumps of sugar belong to our Queen.'

'No, they don't.'

Yes, they do.'

'Well, look,' said the monkey, 'if you tell me what you're doing, I will let you have it.'

'We are conquering the world.'

'What?'

'The world. Conquering it.'

'What for?'

'Because it's there. We have to turn the earth into a gigantic anthill.'

'It's a huge task.'

'Yes,' said the ants looking stern and sad both at the same time. 'We may not accomplish it in our own lifetime. Thank you for the sugar.' They heaved up the lump and made off with it. But one of the ants had remained behind.

'Where are you going?' he asked the monkey.

'To see the world.'

'Can I come with you? Then I could measure it.' The monkey hesitated. What good was an ant for a travelling companion? But she was lonely.

'All right,' she told him. 'You can ride on my shoulder. You'll get a good view and I can carry you easily.' The ant climbed up the monkey's fingers and up her arm till he reached her shoulder. Here he made himself comfortable. 'It is a good view,' he agreed happily.

'Even better from a treetop,' the monkey replied and leaped into the branches. Suddenly the entire tree began to tremble as though in an earthquake. Someone or something was shaking it.

It was an elephant.

'Stop it!' cried the monkey.

'Why?' asked the elephant.

'You're making me sea-sick.'

The elephant stopped it. When the monkey had smoothed down her fur and had made sure that the ant was still on her shoulder, she turned on the elephant, 'Why were you trying to uproot the tree?'

'Well, you see, I'm a good-natured beast.'

'Yes? So what?'

'And the consequence is that I'm taken advantage of. So I was practising getting angry.'

'Oh, was that it? Well, you were doing it wrong.'

'How?'

'Your eyes weren't rolling. You didn't stamp. And you made no noise.'

'Yes,' put in the ant, 'you didn't even bite.'

'I need practice,' said the elephant. She began rolling her eyes. 'It isn't comfortable,' she soon complained and stopped doing it.

'The problem is,' said the monkey, 'you need a good reason to be angry. If you can find a good reason, then it's very likely that your eyes will roll and you will trumpet loudly.'

'What is a good reason?' the elephant wanted to know.

'Provocation,' replied the ant. 'This, for example.' He crawled across to the elephant's forehead and bit her hard between the eyes.

'Was that provocation?' asked the elephant.

'Yes,' said the monkey a little doubtfully.

'What does it mean?'

'It means being attacked without a good reason,' answered the ant.

'Oh. But I don't feel angry.'

The monkey was beginning to feel exasperated. Still she quite liked the elephant. 'Look,' she said, 'why don't you come with us? I'm exploring the world. The ant is measuring it. Perhaps you will find something in the wide world that will make you angry.'

'Oh yes!' cried the elephant, feeling quite pleased to be asked on an adventure. 'That would be splendid.' And so the three of them set off, the monkey on the elephant, the ant on the monkey, and the noonday sun shining on all three.

2

An Important Dream

The grass was sunburnt, yellow and dry. Round, black stones were scattered about. The only trees in sight had been the twisted black ones with silver thorns. Even the sky had turned white at the edges. The monkey and the ant and even the elephant were hot and tired. Luckily, just as they had begun to snap at one another, they noticed a shrine in the distance surrounded by trees. It seemed deserted. On the other side of the shrine, the ground fell away. At the bottom there was a river bed, now almost dry, but with a few puddles still. They washed and drank and ate what they could find, and were soon fast asleep under the trees surrounding the shrine.

That night the monkey dreamed. In her dream the river had nearly overflowed its banks; it was crowded with fish, all of them one-eyed and all of them singing. They were trying to tell her that she had to cross over to the opposite bank. On the other bank she could see a little girl who was feeding the fish. But when the monkey called out to her, the little girl was unable to hear her. She finished feeding the fish and walked away along the river.

The monkey woke up feeling sad. When she had opened her one grey eye, she found a very old woman staring at her. The monkey scrambled to her feet and greeted the old woman. She woke up the others and they all said, 'Good Morning.' The old woman accepted their greetings. 'Why were you calling out in your sleep?' she asked the monkey. The monkey hesitated, then told her what she had dreamt.

The woman looked thoughtful. 'It may be,' she said at last, 'that the three of you might be able to help the little girl. Her name is Aditi. She is the grand-daughter of the King and Queen of this sunburnt kingdom.' The old woman paused. 'Have you noticed,' she asked, 'how hot and arid this country is?'

'Oh yes,' said the elephant and the ant in a heartfelt sort of way. 'We have noticed.'

'Every year,' the old woman went on, 'soon after the rains, a dragon ranges over the entire countryside, sucking up every drop of moisture it can possibly find.'

The ant, the elephant and the one-eyed monkey were listening attentively, their eyes fixed on the old woman's face. 'Last year when the dragon was scorching the palace gardens, the King and Queen pleaded with it. "We will give you anything you want," they said to the dragon, "if only you will promise to go away and never return." The crafty dragon agreed at once. It first made them swear to keep their side of the bargain and then it asked for little Aditi. Well, you can imagine how they felt.'

'What did Aditi think of all this?' demanded the elephant.

'Aditi didn't know. When they told her what had happened, she didn't say anything. She went away to think it over and then she said, yes, she would go. The agreement is that she is to arrive at the dragon's den before the rains and she must not be accompanied by any human being.'

'Has Aditi started on her journey yet?' inquired the monkey.

'She leaves in a week.'

'Poor Aditi,' murmured the elephant. 'If we went with her, perhaps we could help.'

'Yes,' said the ant. 'Let's go with Aditi. I want very much to see a dragon.'

The monkey was looking at the old woman thoughtfully. 'Are you saying that we three might be allowed to go with her?'

'Yes,' replied the woman.

'Where can we find her?'

'You must cross the river. Follow the path there and you will soon come to the walls of a town. Go through the town till you come to a mango grove. Rest there for the night but early the next morning you must make your way to the rose garden. When you find the King and Queen, tell them right away that you will go with Aditi.'

The three were anxious to find Aditi. They breakfasted hurriedly with the old woman. Then they said 'Goodbye' and crossed the river.

3

They Meet Aditi

'But how will we find the rose garden?' The monkey looked worried. They had followed directions with great care and were resting in the mango grove.

'Leave it to me,' answered the ant. 'I will sniff it out.' This he did the following morning by clinging to the tip of the elephant's trunk while she raised it high above the treetops and waved it in the air.

'Let's go,' he shouted. They went through the mango grove and up a short winding path till they came to an expanse of green lawn. Along the edges there were flower beds. Black butterflies with red and white spots

were fluttering about. Four poinsettias were at the four corners and in the centre there was a fountain surrounded by red earth. Near the fountain was a little girl.

'That must be Aditi,' whispered the elephant.

'Yes,' said the monkey trying to decide whether or not they ought to stop. But the little girl had run up to them.

'Hello,' she said.

'Hello. Are you Aditi?'

'Yes.'

The one-eyed monkey, the ant and the elephant introduced themselves. They explained why they had come. There were a number of questions Aditi and the three wanted to ask one another. The ant, in particular, wanted to know about dragons. But he knew it wouldn't do to miss the King and the Queen, so all he said was, 'Can you show us the quickest way to the rose garden?'

Aditi led them and in a short time they reached the garden. The King and Queen were strolling among the roses. Aditi greeted them and introduced the three animals.

The monkey cleared her throat. 'Your Majesties,' she said, 'the ant, the elephant and I have come to offer our services. We will go with Aditi and help her.'

The King and Queen looked a little surprised. 'Thank you,' they said, both very politely, 'but do you know why Aditi has to make the journey and what it's about?'

'Yes,' answered the elephant. 'We will go with Aditi and confront the dragon.'

The King and Queen looked very old and very mournful. But gradually a glimmer of hope began to shine in their eyes as they realised that the one-eyed monkey and the ant and the elephant could go with Aditi. That did not break their bargain with the dragon.

'Will you really go with Aditi?' asked the Queen.

'Yes,' said the ant. 'But you must tell us which way to go.'

'None of us knows where the dragon lives,' answered the King. 'At the other end of the kingdom a sage sits meditating on a small island. It is said of her that she has never lied. If anyone knows, she will know. But she is guarded by three lionesses and six lion cubs.'

'We will ask her,' said the monkey, looking resolute and as though she was ready to set off at once. But the Queen said that they must stay for breakfast and for lunch and for dinner, and indeed, for as long as it took to make proper preparations.

They stayed for three days. The elephant was allowed to roll on the grass, the monkey swung from the great banyans, and the ant investigated the red earth. Aditi ran about and played with each one. In between times they made proper preparations. These included a bag of peanuts, a jar of honey, some dried Bombay duck, a small compass, several maps, a large parasol, and a letter of introduction. The Queen helped them. By the late afternoon of the third day they were nearly done. They were sitting on the lawn drinking tea when the Queen said to them that she and the King had some presents for them which might prove useful. 'Go and fetch your grandfather,' she commanded Aditi. The King joined them and the two old people produced their presents.

The first gift was a cloak of invisibility. The King spread it across the elephant's back and she disappeared. They could see the grass on which she had been sitting and, indeed, still was sitting: it was bent and crushed. The elephant got up and walked about. Then she removed the cloak with the tip of her trunk and bowing low to the King and Queen, she thanked them both.

Next, the King produced a sword. He gave it to the monkey, but the monkey drew back.

'I have never used a sword in my life,' she faltered.

'It is the Sword of Courage,' the King answered quietly. 'You are agile and quick. Use it with caution.'

The monkey accepted the sword from the King and thanked him for it. They stowed it neatly in the parasol handle.

The third gift was a little matchbox. Inside the box was a ball of clay. This the Queen presented to the ant.

'Whatever you make with this clay,' she explained, 'will come into existence. But when you stop concentrating, it will vanish at once.'

The ant set to work making a miniature dragon. When he was done, a huge dragon began to take form. But this so startled him that he stopped concentrating and the dragon disappeared. They were all rather relieved and very impressed. The ant put the clay back into the box and thanked Aditi's grandparents.

They spent that evening with the two old people but rose early the next morning, long before the townspeople were stirring, almost before the birds were up. The King and Queen gave them their blessings and the four adventurers made for the coast.

4

The Journey to the Coast

By noon the next day they had travelled a fair distance,
though the country they were passing through formed
part of a plateau and was hilly and uneven. Aditi and
the monkey had set up the parasol on the elephant's
back and had made a cushion of the cloak. They were
absorbed in conversation.

'Who was the old woman?' the monkey wanted to know.

'Which old woman?'

'The one we met at the shrine by the river.'

'She is my friend,' Aditi answered. 'She used to look after me when I was very little, but now she has retired.'

The monkey was about to tell her how the old woman had interpreted her dream when they heard an outcry and saw a party of villagers they had come upon suddenly fleeing in all directions.

'What caused that?' wondered the elephant.

'I think I know,' answered the ant. 'You see, the cloak we're sitting on has spread out over you and you've become invisible.' And so she had. The one-eyed monkey began to laugh, and was joined by Aditi and the invisible elephant.

'Why are you laughing?' inquired the ant.

'Because,' replied the monkey, 'we must have looked funny, floating through the air with a swaying motion.' After that they adjusted the cloak and stopped for lunch.

'It's a shame about those people,' grumbled the ant. 'I'm absolutely certain we're going the right way but I would have liked to have checked my calculations.' They were headed due west and had covered nearly half the distance.

Aditi and the monkey ate peanuts. The ant nibbled one. The elephant had a few but she knew that even

the whole bagful wouldn't be enough to make a proper meal for her. She wandered off to forage for herself. She ate some grass and the tender leaves from the tops of trees, but she was still feeling hungry so she went a little further. She came upon a farm where the farmer had just finished planting sugarcane. She rooted about and fed happily on the pieces of cane. When she was done, she gathered a few pieces to take to the others. The ant was ecstatic. He gnawed and chewed and chewed and gnawed till he fell asleep. Aditi put him in one of her pockets and they resumed their journey. Suddenly they heard an uproar again. This time it was behind them. It was the farmer and her friends chasing the elephant.

'Quick,' cried the monkey. She draped the cloak over Aditi and herself and spread the edges over the elephant.

'I think we're invisible,' whispered Aditi. 'Walk quietly to the side of the road and then don't move.'

The elephant did exactly as she was told. When the

party of people came to the spot where the elephant had been standing, they didn't know what to do. They stood about and talked a bit and finally went home.

The monkey and the elephant spent the next hour arguing about the rights of the matter. The monkey said that in a way she could understand why those people were angry: after all, they had just planted the cane. But the elephant said that she had been hungry and that the loss of a little sugarcane hurt no one.

The going was mostly downhill now and the countryside seemed greener. The sun was directly in the elephant's eyes and because of this and because of the arguing, she stumbled. The ant woke up, the monkey leaped off. The elephant was in pain: her right forefoot was badly cut.

'Can you rest it on this rock?' asked the monkey. She was feeling sorry she had argued so fiercely with the poor elephant. 'I'll be back in a moment with a little water and we'll bandage your foot.' Aditi got the bandages ready. She and the ant consoled the elephant. Soon the monkey returned. In one hand she carried a coconut shell filled with water and in the other an enormous bunch of ripe bananas. When they had bandaged the elephant's foot and she was feeling better, they ate the bananas and pressed forward.

They reached the coast by sunset. Aditi was tired — she had walked a good bit — and the elephant was limping. But the beach was pleasant, sandy and

deserted. There were a great many palm trees. That
evening the monkey feasted them on tender coconuts.
About a kilometre offshore they could see the island
where the sage lived. The problem was how were they
to get to it without a boat? And what boat would hold
an elephant?

5

The Balloon Fish

Aditi and the monkey had curled up between the elephant's feet. The ant had gone to sleep in his little box. When the sun rose, they all woke up except Aditi. So the elephant rolled over on her back carefully and scrambled up without disturbing Aditi.

But on the beach there was a commotion. The fisherfolk were hauling in last night's catch. Their net was writhing with shrimps and crabs and all sorts of fish. Every now and then they would pick out a fish and toss it on the sand. These fish would lie there looking very unhappy. Eventually, each one would inflate a large balloon at the base of its throat and go on lying there. The one-eyed monkey felt sorry for them. She began to pick them up and toss them into the ocean. The elephant helped her. The fishermen and women didn't like this much but none of them wanted to argue with an elephant, so they didn't say anything.

After a while the fisherfolk left. Aditi woke up and the four adventurers settled down to breakfast (chiefly coconuts). It was then that they heard the voices from the sea. It was the Balloon Fish. They wanted to know how they could thank them. The monkey was saying that it was quite all right and no trouble at all, when the ant interrupted her.

'If you could help ferry the elephant to that island over there, we would be very grateful.'

'All right,' said the fish. 'When the tide has ebbed, wade into the ocean as far as you can. We will meet you there and do our best.'

'Can you swim?' asked Aditi turning to the elephant.

'Only a little,' answered the elephant. 'But I float quite well.'

'Oh good,' they all said.

They spent the morning cutting up vines until they had four hundred lengths of about twenty feet each. By the time they were finished the tide had ebbed. With the ant, the monkey and Aditi on her back, the elephant

waded into the sea. The waves lashed about and her foot hurt. The salt water made the cut sting but it couldn't be helped, so she said nothing. Aditi and the monkey held the lengths of vine. Soon, the water was up to the elephant's shoulders. All about them were hundreds of Balloon Fish. Two hundred fish got under the elephant and helped to buoy her. This tickled a bit but she still said nothing. The remaining fish caught up the ends of the vines between their jaws and began to swim. Aditi and the monkey held on tight. In a very short time they were near the island. They thanked the Balloon Fish. The fish said that it was quite all right and no trouble at all and waved their fins.

When the four adventurers got to the shore, the first thing they did was to see to the elephant's foot. The cut was bleeding but the elephant didn't mind. On the whole she was feeling rather pleased with herself. They walked towards the centre of the island. Suddenly they heard a sharp yelp. The elephant drew back, startled. It was a tiny lion cub. She had nearly stepped on it. She began to tremble. But Aditi picked up the cub and held it in her arms, where it growled and squirmed.

'If you put it down,' suggested the monkey, 'perhaps we could follow it.'

The cub eventually led them to a eucalyptus grove, in the centre of which was a large clearing. In the centre of the clearing there was an exceptionally beautiful cashewnut tree. Under the tree sat the sage. She seemed to be meditating and was surrounded by three lionesses and the rest of the cubs.

'If only we could attract her attention,' whispered the monkey. The three lionesses were looking at them. Their yellow eyes were not friendly.They tried shouting but the sage didn't move and the three lionesses kept staring.

'I'm small,' said the ant, 'so small that I'm nearly invisible. I could slip across and bite the sage to attract attention.'

'No!' cried the monkey but the ant had already entered the clearing and one of the cubs had already seen him. The cub pounced on him. The monkey moved quickly to save the ant but even so he was badly battered.

'We could wait,' said the monkey, 'and have some lunch. She can't go on meditating forever and ever.'

'Yes, she can,' muttered the ant. 'That's what sages do.' They decided that they might as well have some lunch.

6

A Very Bloody Fight and a Little Information

The ant had been badly hurt. He could hardly move. They carried him away tenderly and sat down near a spring. They ate coconuts but they were tired of coconuts and not very hungry and they were all feeling extremely anxious. The elephant, in particular, was very upset. 'I'm bigger than those lionesses,' she thought to herself. 'It's for me to walk past them. If necessary I'll put on the cloak.'

When they had finished eating, she mumbled casually, 'I'm just going off to get a bit more lunch. Wait for me here.' She hurried off in the direction of the grove.

But the ant had guessed what the elephant was thinking. 'Follow her!' he shouted. Aditi grabbed the box in which the ant was lying on a little cotton wool and put it in her pocket. She and the monkey raced after the elephant.

They weren't quick enough. The elephant had tried to walk past the lionesses but in spite of the cloak, they had sensed her presence. Two of them had attacked at once, one on each flank. The cloak of invisibility was torn in half and lay on the ground. The third lioness leapt straight for the elephant's eyes. The elephant flung her aside but the other two lionesses were still clinging to the elephant. Aditi dashed in and tried to retrieve the cloak, but one of the lionesses let go of the elephant and attacked the girl. The monkey intervened, wielding the parasol — she had forgotten about the sword — and dealt the lioness a terrible blow. This enabled Aditi to slip through quickly. She got to the sage and shook her by the shoulders. The elephant,

meanwhile, trumpeted loudly and tossed a lioness high into the air. But the first lioness was back in action. Just as she had sent the monkey flying and was leaping at Aditi, the sage awoke.

All the fighting stopped at once. The lioness tried to stop in mid-air but knocked Aditi down. The one-eyed monkey staggered towards them. She was hurt too. As for the elephant and the three lionesses, they were covered with gore. The lion cubs were also spattered but much of the blood was not their own.

The sage looked at them with her strange eyes which seemed not to see, yet saw anyway.

'You're hurt,' she said. 'Rub your wounds with this ointment right away and come back in an hour.' She gave them a jar of a green, jelly-like substance.

The four friends limped away slowly and washed their wounds. They tried the green ointment. The ant felt better almost at once and after an hour so did Aditi and the one-eyed monkey. It took longest to work on the elephant.

When they appeared before the sage again, no trace of the fight remained. She looked at them serenely.

'What do you wish to know?'

'Where is the dragon's lair, please?' Aditi spoke in a loud clear voice though she felt nervous.

'Which dragon's lair?'

'The one who sucks up all the moisture from the countryside near here.'

'That particular dragon,' answered the sage, 'lives in a cave under the ocean. You must journey southwards till the land ends. At the triangular tip where the oceans converge, there is a large rock. Under the rock is the dragon's cavern.'

'Thank you,' said the four and were about to go away, when the sage spoke again.

'You are welcome to stay here for a day or two and rest if you wish.'

The four adventurers looked at each other, remembering the fight they had had with the lionesses. 'Thank you,' they said, 'but we think perhaps that we had better go.'

The sage looked rueful. 'Very well,' she said. 'I will see you off.' She walked with them to the shore. The elephant was told to face the mainland. The others were told to sit on the elephant's back. The sage then made the elephant rise in the air till she floated a few inches above the ground. 'Goodbye,' called the sage, and gave the elephant a hard push. They drifted slowly across

the ocean. When the four adventurers understood what was happening they shouted, 'Goodbye.' On the far shore they landed gently with a soft thump.

7

On the Beach

They were very tired. They decided to rest by the sea for a day or two before beginning their journey south. On the whole the time was spent pleasantly. They ate, they slept, and they all took turns mending the cloak of invisibility. But there was a little bickering. For one thing, Aditi and the ant scolded the elephant.

'You nearly got killed,' Aditi began.

'You must promise not to do it again,' put in the ant. He was looking at the elephant reproachfully. 'It was silly of you to try to walk past the lionesses alone.'

'Well, that's what you did,' answered the elephant.

'But I was invisible,' returned the ant.

'So was I.'

'No, you weren't. They sensed your presence.'

'Well, you weren't either. The cub attacked you.'

'You were both very silly,' Aditi declared.

The monkey decided it was time to intervene. 'You were both very brave and both very silly,' she said judiciously, hoping to calm them, but the ant and the elephant turned on her.

'You were silly too,' they said to the monkey. 'And so were you,' they added, nodding at Aditi.

'How?' asked the monkey and Aditi together.

'You forgot your sword and you dashed in without any weapons.'

Aditi and the monkey looked abashed. They kept quiet. The ant and the elephant began to feel sorry.

'But you were very brave,' the ant offered.

'Yes, you were. And you dashed in to help me,' added the elephant.

Soon they were in agreement that they had all been rather brave and felt better.

'At least we know where we're going now,' said the ant happily.

'Yes it was a good adventure,' agreed the elephant.

'And we've got some practice for slaying dragons,' added the ant.

'Wait a minute!' exclaimed the monkey. 'Who said anything about slaying the dragon?'

'Well what do you do with a dragon?' inquired the ant.

'We reason with it and try to persuade it that its ways are wrong,' replied the monkey.

'What shall we say?' asked the elephant.

'We'll think of something,' answered Aditi. But they were very tired and fell fast asleep.

The following day the monkey and the elephant went foraging. The ant and Aditi stayed on the beach. It was

a peaceful morning. The tide was coming in. A few gulls floated on the water. The ant was frowning over a packet of maps. Aditi was lying on her back on the sand and watching the clouds and thinking of her grandparents. High overhead she could see a white bird circling slowly. Eventually it descended lower and lower and landed beside them. It was a white falcon.

'I have a letter for you,' the bird said to Aditi, 'and I'm to wait for an answer.'

The letter was from her grandparents asking how she was, and how the others were, and saying that there had been a message from the dragon. The message said that if Aditi did not arrive before the rains began, the dragon would scorch the kingdom to a heap of cinders. Aditi was going to reply at once, but she hadn't any paper.

'If I tell you my letter, will you remember it?' she asked.

'Yes,' said the falcon.

'Well then, here is my letter. "To my grandparents. Thank you for your letter. We are all well. We hope you are well. We know about the dragon and are journeying southwards. With lots and lots of love, Your loving grand-daughter."'

'Is that all?' asked the bird.

'That's all,' replied Aditi. 'Thank you very much.'

So the bird said 'Goodbye' and flew away rapidly with Aditi's letter.

That evening when the other two returned with fruit and nuts, Aditi told them about the message from the dragon.

'We'll have to travel fast,' the monkey responded. She looked worried. But the elephant was indignant.

'We will move fast and we'll teach that dragon a thorough lesson.'

The monkey smiled. 'Are you angry?' she asked.

'No,' said the elephant. 'But it isn't fair, and that dragon needs to be taught a thorough lesson.'

'But you were angry when we fought the lionesses,' said Aditi.

'No, I wasn't angry,' protested the elephant.

'But I heard you trumpet,' put in the ant.

'Yes, and you tossed a lioness high into the air,' added Aditi.

'But I wasn't angry,' insisted the elephant.

'Then why did you do it?'

'What else could I do?' asked the elephant.

The others couldn't think of an answer to this so they began to talk about the journey ahead of them. 'Our best plan,' said the ant, 'is to head south-south-east. We'll have to travel through a jungle but it's the shortest way.'

'I have some relatives in the jungle,' offered the monkey. 'Perhaps they will help us.'

'Good,' said the elephant. 'I have some too.'

But Aditi didn't say anything. She was still wondering what exactly they were going to say to the dragon.

It was decided that they would set out at sunrise the following day. They went to sleep early. But when they woke up the next morning, they found to their dismay that the ant had disappeared.

8

The Kinsfolk

They searched, or rather Aditi and the one-eyed monkey searched. The elephant stayed still, not wanting to step on the ant by accident. But there was nothing to be found except a few peanut shells. The ant and his matchbox with the magic clay had disappeared. Aditi and the elephant couldn't understand it at all but the one-eyed monkey was examining the shells. She looked unhappy.

'I think I know what has happened,' she muttered grimly. But when Aditi and the elephant asked her to explain, she wouldn't answer.

'We must set off at once,' was all she would say, 'and follow this trail of peanut shells into the jungle.'

They marched in silence. The monkey wouldn't take

up any attempts at conversation. By noon they arrived at the fringes of the jungle.

'Wait for me here,' said the one-eyed monkey and leaped into the branches of a gigantic peepal tree. When she got to the top, she let out a complicated and ear-splitting whoop. She returned to the spot where Aditi and the elephant were waiting for her. But when they asked her what she was doing, she still wouldn't answer.

'All I have at the moment are certain suspicions. We'll have to wait and see,' was all she would say.

They sat down to wait. While they were waiting, a black butterfly with red and white spots — exactly like the ones in her grandparents' garden — settled on Aditi's hand. Even as she stared at it, it disappeared. She was quite certain that it hadn't flown away. It had just vanished suddenly. She was puzzled. And then it appeared and disappeared again. As she was thinking about it, a number of monkeys began to enter the clearing by twos and threes.

The one-eyed monkey greeted her relatives. She introduced Aditi and the elephant.

'We are pleased to see you,' said one of the monkeys, 'but why have you summoned us?'

'I have introduced you to two of my friends,' the one-eyed monkey replied gravely, 'but I have a third friend, who is an ant, and he has disappeared.' She went on to tell them about the ant's disappearance together with his matchbox and the piece of clay. As she was nearing the end of her account, some of the monkeys began to leave, but a few remained. The one-eyed monkey looked straight at them and concluded by saying, 'A trail of peanuts shells has brought us here. We seek information.'

The monkeys were looking decidedly embarrassed. Finally, one of them said, 'You have chosen some strange companions for yourself. You are a monkey. An ant is an ant. What has an ant to do with us?'

A few more of the monkeys shuffled away but the one-eyed monkey replied sternly, 'The ant is my friend. He was sleeping peacefully in his matchbox last night beside his clay. When we woke up this morning, he and the matchbox had both disappeared. It is entirely possible that no harm was meant. All we found were the peanut shells. But we want our friend back. Can you help us?'

All the monkeys except one had left. She looked distressed. 'I would like to help you,' she said at last.

'But from what you say, I think you already suspect what it is that has happened. I cannot take your side against the monkey folk but I can give you a clue. The younger monkeys in the royal family are a rowdy lot. They were out last night carousing on the beach. They keep their treasures in a large tamarind tree.' Having said this much, she began to hurry away.

'Wait,' shouted the one-eyed monkey. 'Where is this tamarind tree?'

But the other monkey would not stop. 'I've said all I can,' she whispered rapidly. 'In fact, I think I've already said too much. My first loyalty is to the monkey folk.' She scampered away looking nervous.

'What? Even when they're in the wrong?' the one-eyed monkey called out after her. But the other monkey had fled into the jungle.

The one-eyed monkey felt utterly dejected. She turned to face Aditi and the elephant. 'So now you know what I think has happened.'

'It's not your fault,' said Aditi gently.

'No, it isn't,' put in the elephant. 'If only there was a way the ant could tell us where he is,' she added with a sigh.

'But there is and he has!' cried Aditi suddenly 'While you were talking with the other monkeys, a black butterfly with red and white spots appeared and disappeared. It did this several times. Look! Here it is again!' The black butterfly had settled on her skirt. 'It must be the ant. He has made a butterfly. When his concentration fails, it disappears.'

After that they followed the flickering butterfly very carefully. Within an hour they came in sight of an enormous tamarind tree. They saw the butterfly flutter up to its topmost branches. Several young monkeys were sitting under the tree cracking peanuts and eating tamarinds.

The three friends held a council of war.

'I'm not sure I could uproot that tree, but I could shake it thoroughly,' offered the elephant.

'Oh no, don't do that,' answered the monkey. 'We might lose the ant.'

'We could ask them for the ant,' suggested Aditi.

'What good would that do?' The monkey looked bitter. 'They wouldn't listen.'

'Well, but it was you who said we must reason with the dragon,' put in the elephant.

'Let's try asking,' said Aditi.

So Aditi, the elephant and the one-eyed monkey began to walk slowly towards the group of monkeys under the tamarind.

9

Battling Again

Aditi was in the lead. The young monkeys looked surly but Aditi addressed them politely, 'While we were sleeping on the beach last night, we lost a matchbox. We were hoping you might have found it and will return it to us.'

But the monkeys only jeered. One of them shouted, 'Look, it's a little girl. She has a brown face and no fur at all except on her head. What a funny girl.'

The elephant began to get angry at this. She took a step forward. The monkeys drew back but they continued to jeer. 'We have made a polite request,' the elephant said quietly. 'Will you kindly give us a polite answer?'

'It speaks,' squeaked a monkey. 'That grey, fat bag actually speaks. What else can it do? Let's prod it and see.' Two or three monkeys scampered closer, but the elephant swung her trunk and the monkeys scattered.

The one-eyed monkey was feeling more and more ashamed and angry because of the behaviour of her kinsfolk. 'Stop it!' she shouted. 'You are talking to my friends. Have you no shame, no manners?'

This only made the monkeys turn more ugly. 'Oh look,' they yelled. 'It's the one-eyed monkey come to teach us manners. Let's teach her a lesson!'

A gang of them advanced upon her menacingly. Aditi hit out with the parasol. The elephant wheeled and charged at the monkeys, and the rest of the monkeys joined in the battle. Suddenly there was a thunderous roar. A huge dragon was breathing down on all of them. Its head was higher than the highest treetops. The monkeys ran away squealing with fright. For a moment, Aditi and the elephant and the one-eyed monkey just stood and stared. Then Aditi laughed. 'It's the ant!' she cried. 'Quick, climb up the tree and rescue him at once.' Already the outlines of the dragon were beginning to waver. The one-eyed monkey shinnied up the tree and returned quickly, clutching the matchbox containing the ant. The dragon, meanwhile, had vanished, of course.

The ant was all right, though a little shaken. He would not let them tell him how glad they were that they had found him at last. He wanted to know how they had done it.

'Well, we followed the flickering butterfly,' Aditi told him.

The ant looked pleased. 'I thought you'd catch on,' he said happily.

'And that trick with the dragon was a very good one,' the elephant added. 'It scattered the monkeys.'

The one-eyed monkey was looking about her. 'We had best move on,' she said to the others. 'When the monkeys discover that the dragon is gone, they'll return.'

They walked steadily for the best part of a day till they arrived at the shores of a small lake. They were tired and hungry. None of them had eaten all day. They decided that by now they had travelled far enough and could afford to rest. They ate a little honey and whatever else they could find. Then they made themselves comfortable on the pebbly beach — the ant was in the matchbox and the matchbox was safe in Aditi's pocket — and went to sleep.

They slept soundly. The one-eyed monkey was the first to wake up. The sun was already high in the sky but she didn't feel hot. They seemed to be in the shade and this was surprising since she didn't remember any trees near them. She turned her head. Two large elephants were standing nearby, as though keeping guard. Their bodies shaded the four friends.

10

The Two Elephants

The elephants noticed that the monkey was awake.
They smiled at her. She was somewhat reassured
though still wary. But by this time the others were
awake. When the elephant saw her brothers standing
there, she greeted them joyfully.

'We didn't mean to startle you,' explained the older brother, 'but you looked so tired and were so sound asleep that we thought we would wait.'

The elephant smiled at her brothers. She told them about the trouble with the monkeys. When she came to the bit about the dragon appearing, the younger brother was very impressed.

'Can you make anything at all?' he asked the ant.

'Well, it depends on how well I can imagine it,' replied the ant. He set to work and produced a ball large enough for the elephants to play with. It bobbed on the water. Aditi and the elephants plunged in after it.

The ant and the monkey sat on the beach and watched them play. They were squirting water at the ball with their trunks and each was trying to see who could make it rise higher. Aditi had clambered on her friend's back and was whacking the ball whenever she could get at it. The one-eyed monkey considered joining them but wasn't sure she wanted to get her fur wet. The ant was having fun. Every now and then he would make the ball disappear and reappear.

When they had finished playing, they dried themselves off and the elephant told her brothers regretfully that they had to be on their way.

'Why?' asked her brothers. She explained about the dragon.

'Well, yes, that is important,' the older brother said. But they were all feeling sorry at having to part so soon.

'We'll come with you up to the edge of the jungle,' the younger elephant said.

Everyone thought that this was a splendid idea. They set off happily and within two days they reached the edge of the jungle. But during those two days they had a great deal to think about and a great deal to talk about. The elephants had repeated the question the adventurers themselves had raised earlier: when they found the dragon, what would they say and what would they do? It was hard to answer.

11

What Do You Say to a Dragon?

The ant still assumed that they were going to slay the dragon. He had a notion that that was usually done. The monkey thought differently. She wanted to know the exact wording of the dragon's bargain with Aditi's grandparents. Aditi repeated the gist of it.

'But that would mean that we just leave you with the dragon and go back home. That's ridiculous.' The elephant was indignant.

The monkey interposed. 'All that was promised was that Aditi would appear at the dragon's lair. Once she has appeared, we can all go home.'

'I don't think the dragon will like that much,' the younger elephant said.

'What if the dragon says that's not in keeping with the spirit of the bargain?' the older one asked.

'Well then, we will argue,' the monkey said hotly.

'But how do you argue with a dragon?' asked the elephant.

'Well, let's do a practice run,' said Aditi, who up to this point hadn't said much. 'I'll be me and each of you can take turns being the dragon. We'll start with the ant.' The ant drew himself up and did his best to look like a dragon.

'Greetings O Dragon,' Aditi began. 'In accordance with the agreement between you and my grandparents, I have appeared before you. You, in turn, must cease to ravage my grandparents' kingdom.'

'No,' said the Ant-Dragon.

'What?' said Aditi.

'No. I've got what I want. I have every intention of ravaging your grandparents' kingdom.'

'That's monstrous,' said Aditi.

'You talk too much,' answered the Ant- Dragon. He opened his jaws wide and clamped them shut.

'What did you do?' inquired Aditi.

'I have just opened my jaws wide and swallowed you whole. That's what dragons do. They don't argue. You either have to kill them or they swallow you up.'

'Well, in that case,' said Aditi, who was beginning to get irritated, 'I've just ripped my way through the dragon's stomach.'

'Yes, that's a possibility,' murmured the ant, sounding interested. He took himself off to consider the matter. It was the monkey's turn.

'Greetings,' said Aditi. 'I'm appearing before you as my grandparents promised. All this nonsense about ravaging must stop. And now I'm going home.'

'Greetings,' answered the Monkey-Dragon. 'My understanding was that in exchange for you, I was to stop scorching your grandparents' kingdom. You cannot go home.'

'The word used was "appear",' replied Aditi.

'That is true,' said the Monkey-Dragon, 'but if you recall the earlier part of the bargain, I was distinctly offered anything I wanted and I asked for you.'

'But I can't be owned. I'm not an object,' replied Aditi indignantly.

'That's as may be. But now that I've got you, I'm going to keep you.'

'You can't,' shouted Aditi.

'I can,' shouted the Monkey-Dragon.

Then they both stopped. The monkey looked rueful. 'If dragons argue,' she said, 'we might win our case, but it would take several years.' She went off to think. It was the elephant's turn. But the elephant said that she would be Aditi and Aditi could be the dragon.

The elephant began, 'This business about ravaging people's kingdoms is all wrong. You must stop it at once.'

'Why?' asked the Aditi-Dragon.

'Because it's cruel and unjust.'

'Nonsense. What is, is. And what is, is just.'

'That's nonsense,' said the elephant. 'It's wrong to destroy or hurt others.'

'I shall do as I please,' answered the Aditi-Dragon. 'Who shall stop me?'

'I shall,' answered the elephant.

'How?' asked the Aditi-Dragon.

'If necessary I shall kill you.'

'But you just said that it's wrong to destroy or hurt others,' murmured the Aditi-Dragon.

The elephant got so angry she trumpeted loudly. Aditi had to stop and calm her down.

Her two brothers, who had been listening to all this, were also upset. 'It's best to be as well prepared as possible,' they counselled. 'Have you any weapons?' The elephant told them about the sword and the cloak and the magic clay.

'That's good,' they said, but they still looked worried when they said 'Goodbye' on the fringe of the jungle.

The four adventurers continued southwards. According to the ant, a day's journey would bring them to the dragon.

12

Beautiful by Moonlight

They walked rapidly all that day, paying no attention to the green paddy-fields or the red earth, to the small hills or the large boulders. Their minds were intent on the dragon's cave; they kept trying to imagine what would happen. By sunset they were within a kilometre of their destination. In the distance they could see a large rock. The land narrowed to a triangular tip. All about them they could hear the ocean. They called a halt and consulted with one another.

The elephant wanted to push on ahead and have it out with the dragon but the ant suggested that it might be better to reconnoitre first. The one-eyed monkey said she would go.

'There's only one cloak,' she added, 'so I'll go alone.'

'No, I'll bring the sword,' Aditi insisted.

But the elephant and the ant felt left out. In the end they decided they would all go.

'Let's wait till it's dark,' Aditi suggested, 'and have dinner first.' They were all feeling terribly excited and found it difficult to eat. Soon it was dark. A crescent moon had risen in the sky. But they made themselves wait for at least an hour before they set out.

They walked silently and quietly in the dark. The elephant, in particular, was very careful. Even so, every now and then, a twig would crackle. When they got to the rock, they saw that the ground fell away to a beach. The ocean roared and gleamed below. At another time they might have admired the view but now they were more interested in the crack of light showing under the rock. They pressed close and peered down. The dragon was sprawled in a large cave lit by phosphorescence. Smaller caves led off from the central one. These were spilling over with treasures and junk. The dragon itself had closed its eyes and was breathing gently.

'It's a green dragon,' whispered Aditi. And indeed, in that light, its scales shone a greenish blue.

'No, that's just the light,' answered the ant. The dragon stirred.

'Where shall we hide if the dragon wakes up and comes out of the cave?' asked the elephant. In their excitement they had forgotten the cloak.

'Below the cliff,' replied the monkey. 'But I don't think it will wake up. Look, it's already beginning to snore quietly.'

Just then a little water rushed into the cave. It curled and lapped around the sleeping dragon. The dragon seemed to like this. It squirmed luxuriously. Then it woke up. Its eyes were like cauldrons filled with glowing coals. It lumbered to its feet. Its head grazed the top of the cave.

'That dragon's going to be difficult to slay,' the ant whispered.

The dragon scratched itself and shook off the water. It prepared to climb out through the roof of the cave.

Slowly the rock lifted. The four adventurers scurried to the cliff and lowered themselves to a ledge below.

The dragon slithered up through the mouth of the cave and rolled the rock back. Then it took a short run towards the cliff edge and glided away over the ocean.

They breathed once again. The dragon had taken off directly overhead but luckily for them, it hadn't noticed them.

They watched the flying dragon. The ant had been right. In the moonlight it shone gold and silver. Every now and then it would beat its wings. Then the light would slide and glitter on its scales. It was magnificent. Still, the four adventurers were very frightened. They made their way back and fell into a restless and anxious sleep. They knew that the following morning they would have to face the dragon.

13

Inside the Cave

The sun had risen. They walked steadily towards the dragon's rock. They had the cloak, they had the sword, and they had the magic clay. Aditi was rehearsing a speech in her head. This time no peering or hiding for them: Aditi picked up a stone and rapped on the rock. Nothing happened. Aditi knocked harder; the others took turns. They tried shouting. After fifteen minutes, when they were all quite hoarse, the rock lifted and the dragon poked its head out sleepily.

'If you don't stop that racket,' it said briefly, 'I will eat you up.' It went back into the cave and pulled the rock back.

The four were uncertain about what to do next. Finally Aditi decided that since they had woken the dragon, they might as well go on.

'Greetings O Dragon,' she shouted down the crack. 'We have business with you. Please return.'

The dragon appeared, looking very irritable.

'I am Aditi,' Aditi began.

The dragon interrupted. 'Good,' it said. 'Who are these animals? Are they any use? Well, we'll see.' Before they knew it, Aditi, the elephant and the one-eyed monkey had been scooped into the cave and the rock rolled back. The ant was perched on the monkey's shoulder but the dragon had not noticed him.

Inside the cave the dragon sprawled out. 'I'm going to sleep for an hour or two. When I wake up, I will set you your tasks.'

'But,' said the elephant. 'But,' said the ant, Aditi and the monkey. It was useless. Anything they had to say was entirely drowned by the dragon's snores.

The four adventurers huddled together. Things weren't going at all as they had planned. They were all annoyed by the dragon's behaviour.

'I don't think this dragon will listen,' said the elephant.

'No, it won't,' put in the ant. 'The sensible thing to do would be to slay it now, while it's still fast asleep and we still can.'

'It seems fairer to challenge it first,' answered the elephant.

'But it's not a fair fight. I'm not sure that even the four of us could kill this dragon.'

'Well, we fought the three lionesses and six lion cubs.'

'But what are three lionesses and six lion cubs in comparison to a dragon?'

Aditi and the monkey had been listening to this conversation with increasing anxiety. The monkey spoke. 'I think it's more reasonable to try to talk to it first.'

Aditi seconded her. 'We ought, at least, to give it a try. Besides, if we kill the dragon, we'll be trapped in here. How can we get out? The entrance is too high and the rock is heavy.'

They decided to wait until the dragon woke up and

try to reason with it. Meanwhile, it seemed sensible to explore the smaller caves to see if they could discover some means of getting out.

In addition to the central cave there were three others. The first of these was filled with metal, broken sword blades, old horseshoes, copper vessels, golden chains, silver chains, iron chains, innumerable nails and rusty armour. It led nowhere. The second cave was filled with glass, some of it broken, some intact, thousands of beads, pearls, emeralds and diamonds. Like the first, it was a dead end. The third cave was slippery and slimy and filled with seaweed and broken fishing nets and shrimps and oysters. It turned into a tunnel which led to the ocean. But as the tunnel progressed, it became much too narrow to admit the monkey, much less the elephant.

They returned to the cave in which the dragon was sleeping. By this time it had woken up.

'What I want you to do,' it said to Aditi, 'is to cook and clean and look after the cave. You can be my servant.'

'No,' said Aditi. 'That's not why we are here. You must listen.'

But the dragon wasn't listening. It was looking at the one-eyed monkey doubtfully. 'Too skinny to eat,' it muttered to itself, 'and probably too tough.'

'Look here,' said the monkey, 'it is not our function to serve you, you know.'

But the dragon interrupted. 'Can you write?' it asked.

The monkey was so startled, she replied without thinking, 'Yes, I can.'

'Good,' said the dragon. 'I'll dictate and you take dictation. I'm writing the story of my life, you know.' Then it instructed the elephant to help Aditi with the heavier housework.

The elephant said, 'No,' very loudly and for once the dragon heard.

'Speak when you're spoken to and don't interrupt,' it said sharply. The elephant was about to charge the dragon but Aditi and the ant stopped her. The ant had still not been noticed by the dragon. Meanwhile, the dragon had grabbed the monkey in one of its paws and was telling her to write.

'I,' began the dragon, 'was born in an egg. I grew and grew till I cracked it open. I then found myself in a huge cave but I ate shrimps and seaweed till I grew strong enough to burst through the top. I am the biggest dragon in the world. And when I grow large enough I shall crack the sky.'

Aditi and the elephant were listening to this in astonishment. They wanted to giggle but did not dare. The dragon was looking extremely pleased. 'There,' it said, 'isn't that splendid? Tomorrow we will do the second chapter.' Suddenly it roared, 'Where is my supper?'

'What would you like for supper?' asked Aditi sweetly. She had decided that for the time being it was probably best to humour the dragon. They needed time to think of a plan. Besides, it was holding the monkey in one of its paws and it seemed unwise to irritate it further.

By now the dragon's stomach was growling. 'Seaweed soup,' it snapped at Aditi. 'Don't ask stupid questions.' It found that it was still holding the monkey. 'Here, you go and help,' it said to the monkey. 'And if there's anything left, you can share the left-overs.' It flung the monkey in their direction.

The one-eyed monkey hit the floor near their feet. She was stunned and bruised and her head was bleeding. This was too much for the other three. Aditi drew the Sword of Courage and challenged the dragon.

14

Sword Blades and Fishing Nets

Even so, everyone was startled. The ant, who was sitting in his matchbox in a corner, had been expecting a fight but this was rather sudden. He set to work on the ball of clay with furious concentration. But it was really the dragon who was most taken aback. At first it didn't understand at all what was happening. When it realised that Aditi was actually challenging it, it began to laugh. While it was busy roaring with laughter, the one-eyed monkey ran out of the cave and into the one that led to the ocean. This only made the dragon laugh harder.

'You and who else?' it jeered at Aditi.

Aditi thought that she had seen the elephant out of the corner of her eye but now even the elephant had disappeared. For a moment it looked as though her friends had deserted her but Aditi couldn't believe this. She did not waver.

'We're going to fight you,' she said steadily. 'You leave us no choice.'

Suddenly the dragon lashed out at Aditi but Aditi was too quick for it and slashed its paw. The sight of its own blood appalled the dragon. In all its life no one had ever fought it before. They had all been too frightened.

While the dragon was gazing at its dripping claw and Aditi was wondering what to do next, the monkey returned, dragging in fishing nets. She began to fling these over the dragon. It roared indignantly. Luckily for them it was much too large to move easily within the cave and now it was further hampered by being tangled in the nets.

It began to puff itself up slowly. The elephant, who was wearing the cloak of invisibility, guessed at once what the dragon was going to do. Before it could send out a sheet of fire, she charged the dragon and got it in the stomach. The dragon collapsed with a terrible groan but the elephant's back had been ripped by its claws and the cloak, as usual, had fallen to the ground. The elephant wheeled and was preparing to charge the dragon again, and Aditi and the monkey were piling on fishing nets, when they heard an angry buzzing overhead. A swarm of bees was heading straight for the dragon's nose. As the first bee hit, the dragon let out an anguished yelp. It swung its head wildly. There was a crack like thunder. The dragon slumped. It had hit its head on the roof of the cave and knocked itself out.

Aditi and the monkey, with the elephant helping, were piling on nets. The bees had disappeared. They could hear the ant shouting, 'Tie it securely!' When they had done so, Aditi picked up the fallen sword and trimmed the dragon's claws one by one. Then they stood back and admired their handiwork.

'Well, perhaps now the dragon will listen to reason,' the monkey remarked.

The ant's trick with the bees had worked beautifully. They congratulated him, then settled down to rest and munch on seaweed till the dragon recovered.

15

What the Dragon Said

After a while the dragon opened its eyes slowly. Aditi
gave it a little water. When the dragon had regained
consciousness, they confronted it.

'Now,' asked the monkey, 'will you listen to reason?'

'No,' roared the dragon.

'Very well then, we will leave you here.' This was
the elephant.

'You can't escape,' roared the dragon.

'Yes, we can,' answered the ant. 'We'll pile all the
treasure and junk on top of you and clamber up. The

elephant can easily push back the rock.'

The dragon was silent. At least it said, more quietly this time, 'Well, what do you want?'

'We want you to stop scorching the countryside.' Aditi's voice was very firm. 'Why do you do it?'

'I do it for fun. I get bored flying about all by myself. Besides, I like the attention.'

'Haven't you any friends?' inquired the monkey.

'No,' said the dragon. 'I've lived in this cave all my life. I don't know anyone.'

'What about the damage you do to other people? Don't you care about that?' asked Aditi.

'No,' replied the dragon. 'I don't think about other people. I only think about myself.'

'I always have,' it added simply.

'No wonder,' remarked the elephant.

'No wonder what?' asked the dragon.

'No wonder you haven't any friends,' explained the elephant.

'Well, I'd like to have friends,' said the dragon.

'In order to have friends you have to be friendly,' the one-eyed monkey told the dragon.

'How?' asked the dragon.

For a moment the four adventurers couldn't think of what to say. At last the ant said, 'Well, you have to think of other people.'

'But I don't know how,' replied the dragon.

The elephant was beginning to feel sorry for the

dragon. 'You could learn how,' she said to the dragon.

The dragon kept quiet. Suddenly it said, looking straight at the four adventurers, 'Would you be willing to be friends with a dragon?'

They all felt awkward, particularly the elephant. She didn't really like the dragon very much and she felt that it still had a lot to learn.

At last Aditi said, 'No, not yet. You haven't behaved in a way that would make us like you very much. But we'll take you to an island. If the sage will have you, you can live there and look after the lion cubs. That way you'll get some practice thinking about others.'

'But will I like the island?' asked the dragon doubtfully.

'I don't know,' said Aditi, 'but at least you won't be all alone.'

'All right,' said the dragon. 'Take me there.'

'You have to say "please",' remarked the elephant.

'Why? All right, please take me there.'

'Do you promise to try to think of other people?' the monkey asked.

'And to stop scorching my grandparents' kingdom?' Aditi added.

'Yes,' said the dragon.

'Just a minute,' the ant interrupted. 'We'll have to think it over.' The four withdrew to discuss the matter.

'If we release the dragon,' the ant pointed out, 'we have no guarantee that it won't turn unpleasant.'

'We're taking a chance,' agreed the monkey, 'but it does seem willing to learn.'

'After all, its claws are trimmed,' Aditi said.

'Yes, let's give it a chance,' the elephant put in. 'It seems willing to go to the island.'

They returned to the dragon and began

disentangling it from the fishing nets. When this was done, they all clambered out. The adventurers and the dragon blinked in the sunlight. The dragon stretched and spread its wings.

'You know, we saw you flying in the moonlight last night,' the elephant told it. 'You looked beautiful.'

'Did I really?' The dragon sounded surprised and pleased. It was the first compliment it had ever had. It preened a little. After a moment it said shyly — it hadn't had much practice being pleasant — 'Would you like me to fly you to the island?'

The four adventurers looked at one another. They had all wondered what it would be like to fly with the dragon.

'Yes, please,' they said, 'and thank you very much.'

16

The Return

They were several hundred feet up in the air on the dragon's back. Below them stretched the blue ocean. On their right they could see the line of the coast. The ant was delighted. 'It's like a map!' he cried. 'This way I could draw the map of the world.' They were enjoying themselves though the elephant felt nervous whenever the dragon banked. Soon it began to descend lower and lower. Within an hour they had reached the island.

They approached the clearing. The dragon had made itself as small as possible. This time the lionesses remained motionless and the sage opened her eyes at once.

'Well?' she asked.

'We have brought you the dragon,' Aditi explained. 'It wants to learn.'

The sage extended her right hand and stroked the dragon. The dragon purred. It had rather a gentle purr. The six lion cubs crawled under its stomach.

'Would you like to stay,' asked the sage, 'and look after the cubs?'

'Yes,' said the dragon. 'Please,' it added.

'Very well,' said the sage, 'but first you must fly your friends home.'

'They're not my friends yet,' muttered the dragon.

'But they will be if you work at it,' replied the sage. 'All things considered, they have been quite nice to you, have they not?'

'All right,' said the dragon. 'If they would like me to, I will fly them home.'

So the four adventurers and the dragon set off again. Within ten minutes they were hovering over the palace gardens. There was no one to be seen except Aditi's grandparents. All the others were hiding in their houses.

'I think they are frightened of me,' said the dragon mournfully. 'They don't know I've changed. I'll set you down and leave at once.'

'Thank you,' said Aditi. 'Perhaps when we've told them, you can come and visit us.'

'Can I really?' asked the dragon.

'Yes,' they all said. 'And we'll come and visit you. We'll see each other often.'

The dragon was smiling as it waved goodbye. Then the four adventurers greeted Aditi's grandparents. They had been standing there listening in astonishment to this conversation with the dragon.

'What happened?' they both asked. 'And how glad we are to see you.' They kissed and hugged them in turn and made them recount all their adventures. When the townspeople learnt that Aditi had returned and that the dragon would not trouble them any more, they too were overjoyed. There was a great celebration throughout the kingdom and much merrymaking and lots of firecrackers.

When things had settled down, Aditi, the elephant and the ant thought that they could live peacefully ever after, but the one-eyed monkey shook her head wisely. She proved to be right. There's a penalty attached to dealing with dragons. The four adventurers were often called upon to give their help, and since they were helpful, they often gave it. In the course of time they had a great many adventures. But even so, when they were much older and possibly wiser, they sometimes looked back on this particular adventure and spoke of how they had first met and become friends with one another.

OTHER BOOKS IN THE **SIMPLY A STORY** SERIES

Aditi and the Thames Dragon *by Suniti Namjoshi*
That Summer at Kalagarh *by Ranjit Lal*

Aditi and the One-Eyed Monkey (English)

© Suniti Namjoshi (text)
© Bindia Thapar (illustrations)
First published by Sheba Feminist Publishers, London, 1986.
First published in India, 2000
First reprint, 2002
ISBN 81-86896-14-7
Rs 80.00

printed and bound at
The ind-com press, 393 Velachery Main Road, Vijaynagar,
Velachery, Chennai 600 042

distributed by
Goodbooks Marketing Pvt. Ltd., 76 Fourth Street,
Abhiramapuram Chennai 600 018, India
email goodbuks@vsnl.com website: goodbooksindia.com

published by
Tulika Publishers, 13 Prithvi Avenue, Abhiramapuram, Chennai 600 018, India
email kaka@tulikabooks.com & tulbooks@md4.vsnl.net.in
website: www.tulikabooks.com